THE RAVEN AND THE LOON

Published by Inhabit Media Inc. • www.inhabitmedia.com

Inhabit Media Inc. (Iqaluit). P.O. Box 11125. Iqaluit. Nunavut. X0A 1H0 • (Toronto). 146A Orchard View Blvd.. Toronto. Ontario. M4R 1C3

Editors: Neil Christopher and Kelly Ward
Art director: Danny Christopher

We acknowledge the support of the Canada Council for the Arts for our publishing program.

Printed in Guangzhou. China by Global Printing. Sourcing & Development. Ltd. August 2014. #45551

Canada Council   Conseil des Arts
for the Arts   du Canada

Library and Archives Canada Cataloguing in Publication

Qitsualik-Tinsley. Rachel. 1953-. author
        The raven and the loon / written by Rachel and Sean
Qitsualik-Tinsley.

ISBN 978-1-927095-50-8 (bound)

        I. Qitsualik-Tinsley. Sean. 1969-. author II. Title.

PS8633.I88R39 2013   jC813'.6   C2013-903149-9

THE RAVEN AND THE LOON

BY RACHEL AND SEAN QITSUALIK-TINSLEY

ILLUSTRATED BY KIM SMITH

INHABIT
MEDIA

There was Raven.

There was Loon.

Both were plain white.

They were stuck without colour.

Raven hated anything boring.

And without colour, he bored even himself!

He flew back.

He flew forth.

Really, he was trying not to go crazy with boredom.

Then he spotted Loon's iglu.

Loon was sewing when Raven burst in.

Nobody really liked Raven.

But Loon was patient.

"Flying anywhere, Raven?" asked Loon politely.

"Back, forth," said Raven with a shrug. "But now I'm here! I'll keep you company!"

As usual, Raven talked.

And talked.

Loon sewed.

She listened.

Until Raven ran out of things to say.

Bored, Raven pointed to Loon's sewing and said, "I could do better than that!"

Loon grew angry at Raven's rudeness.

Loon was about to shout at Raven.

But then Raven suddenly said, "Wait! I'm brilliant! I know what we can do for each other. I'll make a pretty coat for you, and you make one for me. Yes?"

Loon had to admit that her own coat bored her.

So, Raven took Loon's needle and her precious stone lamp.

Raven used his magic.

He dipped the needle in lamp soot.

"Sit still," he told Loon.

Loon sat while Raven painted her with magic strokes.

Wherever the needle touched her feathered coat, the soot left

amazing patterns.

"I'm beautiful!" cried Loon, once the painting was done.

She turned in a circle, loving her new coat.

Raven was proud.

He could not stop praising his own work.

Loon took the needle.

She made Raven sit.

She knew she could do a better job.

If only Raven would be still!

While Loon painted Raven, his mouth kept moving.

She shushed him.

He barely heard her.

Worse, Raven jerked all over the place.

How could Loon make her perfect pattern while silly Raven was
so excited?

For the hundredth time, Raven jerked.

The needle zigzagged.

Loon's beautiful work was ruined.

Loon became angry.

"You've ruined it!" she yelled.

Loon threw her lamp at Raven.

The black soot covered him.

Raven stood in shocked silence.

From head to toe, he was black!

Anger rose in him.

Raven picked up Loon's stone lamp.

He threw it at her feet.

It hit Loon hard, mashing her feet completely flat.

Grumbling and calling each other names, Raven and Loon left each other.

But animals like that have long memories.

To this day, ravens have kept their black feathers, and loons have kept their flat feet.

Don't judge Raven and Loon too harshly.

After all, none of us were there.

What's said about them might just be gossip.

And at least Loon has her pretty feathers.

And at least Raven . . . well, he's never bored.

Rachel Qitsualik-Tinsley

Rachel is of the people who call themselves Inuit. She grew up dogsledding across the Arctic, living in snow houses, and watching her father fight off polar bears. She worked for a long time to help other cultures understand her people. She's bursting with stories to tell. And no matter how many she's already told, she just can't tell enough. She eventually told so many stories that the Queen of England gave her a medal for it. For her, the Arctic is wise and alive. If you don't understand that, visit and find out for yourself!

Sean Qitsualik-Tinsley

Sean is from a mixed background. He tells a lot of stories, but he likes hearing them even better. He studies myths and folktales and fables from all around the world. When he can't get enough, he makes up his own! He even tells stories about things that might happen in the far future. That's how, one day, he got an award for writing science fiction. He loves nature and thinks the Arctic is the most beautiful place he's ever seen. So he tries to treasure it by writing about the Arctic's beauty in stories.

Kim Smith

Kim has worked in magazines, advertising, animation, and children's gaming. She has illustrated two picture books with Inhabit Media. She studied illustration at the Alberta College of Art and Design in Calgary, Alberta, where she currently resides.

·WWW.INHABITMEDIA.COM·